CHILDREN'S TELEVISION WORKSHOP

CHELLI TELLS THE TRUTH

WRITTEN BY
SARAH ALBEE

ILLUSTRATED BY
CAROL O'MALIA

As seen on

CARTOON NETWORK

A GOLDEN BOOK • NEW YORK

Published by Golden Books Publishing Company, Inc.,
in cooperation with Children's Television Workshop

A portion of the money you pay for this book goes to Children's Television Workshop.
It is put right back into BIG BAG, SESAME STREET, and other CTW educational projects. Thanks for helping!

One day, Chelli and Bag were playing in the park. Suddenly Chelli stopped and looked around.

"Did you hear something, Bag?" he asked. Chelli looked up into the tree above them. "It sounds like meowing, Bag!"

"It's a kitten, Bag!" cried Chelli. He climbed onto a park bench and lifted a black and white kitten off a branch. "Oh, Bag! I've always wanted a kitten!" Chelli glanced around quickly. "No one seems to be looking for him. I will keep him!"

"What's that, Bag?" Chelli asked. "You think I should look harder for his owner? Well, okay." Chelli sighed. Then he turned around in a slow circle. "I don't see anyone looking for a kitten, Bag. He must have run away. Oh, my very own beautiful kitten! I will name him Bill."

Chelli scratched Bill behind the ears.

"*Purrr,*" said Bill.

"I will buy you a collar," said Chelli. "And I will feed you your favorite foods—cat munchies, milk, anything you want."

Chelli reached into Bag and pulled out some yarn for Bill to play with. Chelli was so excited about the kitten, he didn't notice that Bag was frowning at him.

Kim walked by with some friends. "Is that a new kitten, Chelli?" she cried. "He's so cute! Who gave him to you?"

"Uh, well, you see, it was like this . . . ," said Chelli. Then he tried again. "He wasn't exactly given to me. Not exactly." Chelli's tummy started to feel funny, but he didn't know why.

"Bag and I have to go now," said Chelli. "We're going to make a bed for Bill at Molly's store."

And off went Chelli and Bag.

At the store Chelli found some soft rags. He was putting them into a shoe box when Molly came out, carrying her purse.

"Hi, Chelli! Hi, Bag!" said Molly. "What are you making?"

Chelli hid the box from Molly. "Oh, uh, nothing, Molly!" he stammered. "It's a . . . uh . . . surprise!" He reached inside his jacket and stroked Bill's head, hoping he wouldn't meow. Chelli's tummy felt funny again.

"Well, have fun!" said Molly. She put a sign on the door that said BE BACK SOON and went to run an errand.

Chelli stroked Bill's fluffy fur. "I'm sure no one is looking for you," he said. "I bet you were trying to find a new home when I came along. Right?"

"Maybe you came from a faraway jungle," Chelli continued. "You were taking a catnap in a banana tree, and somebody picked your bunch of bananas and put you on a ship. Maybe you had just arrived when I found you, and you were scared, and it was a good thing I came along. Right, Bill?"

Bill purred.

"Or maybe you ran away from the circus," Chelli went on. "Maybe you had to wear a silly costume and ride around on an elephant, and you hated it so you ran away. Well, I'll take good care of you. No silly costumes for you, Bill."

Bill yawned.

"Or maybe . . ." Chelli stopped. He looked down sadly at the little kitten, who was playing. Then he looked at Bag.

"Oh, Bag, it's no use," wailed Chelli. "I can't keep Bill. I bet he has an owner, and that person is very sad right now. We have to try really hard to find his owner."

Chelli's friend Bag was smiling.

Just then, Molly walked in and set down her bags.

"There's something I have to tell you, Molly!" cried Chelli. "This kitten doesn't belong to me! I wanted to keep him, but I know that wouldn't be right." Chelli started to sniffle.

Molly put an arm around him. "Thank you for telling me the truth, Chelli," she said. "I'm proud of you. Come on. I'll help you and Bag make some signs to put up."

Chelli and Bag hung signs all around the neighborhood.

That night, Chelli put Bill to bed. "Good
night, Bill," he said softly. "Maybe we'll find
your owner tomorrow. . . ."

The next day, Chelli and Bag were playing with Bill near the tree where they had found him. Suddenly they heard a girl's voice cry, "BUSTER!!"

A little girl rushed over to Bill's box. She picked Bill up and kissed him over and over.

Then the girl turned to Chelli and Bag. "You must be the ones who found Buster. Thank you so much."

Chelli felt glad and sad all at once. "I really wanted a kitten," he whispered. "I wanted to keep him, but I knew that would be wrong. I named him Bill."

The little girl hugged Chelli. "It must have been really hard to give him up," she said softly. "Thanks for taking care of him."

"You and Bag can come to our house anytime to play with him," the little girl went on.

Chelli bent down to pat the kitten.

"And you know what else?" said the girl. "I'm going to give him a new name."

Chelli, Bag, and Buster all looked at her in surprise. The little girl smiled and said, "From now on, I'm going to call him Buster Bill!"